FIRST WATCH

BY KATHLEEN STICKNEY
ILLUSTRATIONS SOPHIA SCULL

outskirts
press

"The Earth is what we all have in common."

Wendell Berry

TABLE OF CONTENTS

ALONE

For most of his cat life, Max had no friends. He preferred it that way. When he was very small, he learned that black cats brought bad luck. He came to understand that "unlucky" translated to "unwanted". He became comfortable alone. It was simpler.

As they grew, his sisters and brothers pounced and rolled. Their fur coats sported stripes, spots and colors. They played and fluttered like happy butterflies. When families began to visit, looking to adopt, adults and children laughed and reached out to touch. But when Max tumbled into view the happy conversation slowed.

"Too bad really but a lot of folks think black cats are bad luck," someone would say.

Or perhaps, "Now that's a real Halloween cat

When he was very small, he learned that black cats brought bad luck.

you got there. Looks like something a witch might take home."

And once, worse still, "That one is creepy."

As the weeks passed, it was always the same when people looked at Max.

"We are looking for a more colorful pet."

"No, not that one. Let me see your other kittens."

And so it went, until slowly all of Max's brothers and sisters joined new families. Left behind, he consoled himself with the thought that at least he would remain in the house where he was born. But that was not to be.

Max arrived at the animal shelter on a rainy Saturday. It was a place of clanging metal doors and barking dogs. He sat quietly inside a wet cardboard carrier, after a hasty drop-off. There were no goodbyes. At the intake desk, a stooped man with white hair and a wool fisherman's sweater pulled open the box. He lifted Max out onto a table.

"Uh-oh. Another one. Darn. You guys are hard to get rid of," he murmured, and then called down a long cement corridor, "Dorothy, just got another black cat." He began tapping on a keyboard.

Max watched.

"Poor little fella. Not your fault that folks aren't looking for black cats, and they aren't looking for 'fierce.' They want cuddly."

The keyboard clicked rapidly.

"Age? Weight? Name? Nothing here to tell me you got a name yet."

A female voice drifted down the hall, "Sven, just get the check-in done, will ya? Any slower up there and I'm moving you to cage cleanup."

Sven's fingers moved to scratch under Max's chin, "In some parts of the world I've been to, black cats bring good luck. You'd be something special if you were born in say, Scotland or Japan." He turned back to his computer, "But in this harbor town, a cat like you needs a shield. And the right name can be a shield."

The female voice called again, "Move it! Get that animal entered into the computer. No one cares what name you give it."

Listening, Max blinked. For a moment, with

amber eyes closed, he was only darkness. He seemed to vanish, melting into the shadows at the edge of the desk.

"Ok, that is unnerving," Sven muttered, staring hard.

Max opened his eyes again and looked directly at the old fisherman.

Looking relieved, the man continued, "You deserve a strong name. A name that tells the world you're coming. I'm going to call you Maximus. You'll be a namesake of gladiators and Roman soldiers."

And with a few more clicks on the keyboard, Max officially became Max.

Check-in complete, Sven picked up the new arrival and carried him past rows of caged animals. A barred door hinged open and he deposited Max on a cement floor.

"Just keep those eyes open, Maximus," Sven said as his footsteps receded.

Max turned to face the curious appraisal of his cellmates. All the faces looking at Max were young. Very young. As he sat there, the faces began to shuffle toward him. A dozen kittens jostled each other, forming an irregular circle. Silence reigned. They inched closer, eyes wide, unblinking. One of the kittens tromped directly on Max's tail and still they moved closer. Max brought himself up to his full standing height. The circle tightened and the stare-down continued.

"Boo!" barked a loud voice.

The kittens jumped and scattered like leaves. Max swung his head back toward the door. He found himself staring directly into the mouth of a brown bear. Heart racing, he took in the square head and the teeth. Many teeth. Rooted to the floor, his fur puffed and bristled. He doubled in size. Instinctively, his body curved sideways, profile broadening, tail switching.

"Name's Flint. I'm just across the way from you," the bear said.

As the words sank in, Max realized that the creature before him was not actually in the same room with him. In fact, it stood in a kennel across a narrow hallway, with not one, but two barred doors between them. His heartbeat slowed and his fur began to relax. He took a closer look.

"I'm a Rottweiler if that's what you're wondering," the bear said. "A Rottweiler is a breed of dog. Not everyone knows that."

Continuing on he said, "You'll be fine in here. Decent food. Warm. A bit crowded in your room though," and he glared with annoyance at the kittens that had already forgotten about Max.

"Thanks," said Max curtly, his fur smoothing out.

"Like I said, my name's Flint. What should I call you?"

Max shook his head, "Just got a name. It's Maximus, I guess. Uh, just Max actually."

"Well, glad you arrived," Flint continued, pushing his nose through the bars of his door. You seem a bit older than the rest of the sand fleas in there with you. They come and go so fast, I don't bother keeping track of 'em. Been here three months myself. Long time. Not many families looking for a full grown dog my size," he said and fell quiet.

"Name's Flint. I'm just across the way from you," the bear said.

Over the next few weeks, Max adjusted to the routine of the shelter. The door squeaked open morning and evening at mealtime. Every day people arrived to take a look, and sometimes they took kittens home. Max made an effort to join the kittens crowding around the visitors.

Watching from across the hall, Flint called out friendly advice, "Max, hey you, Maximus! Come out into the light where the children can see you." Or, "Open those eyes wider. If I can't see you, they can't see you."

Max listened and took Flint's suggestions to heart. No luck though. Colorful kittens came and went. But not Max. Max stayed.

Weeks passed and Max grew older. He became less cuddly every day. Flint continued to call from across the hall, but Max withdrew. He stopped exchanging even a few words with Flint. The Rottweiler persisted, but he might as well have been talking to himself. Silent Max had come to a decision. He needed to get used to being alone. It was his future.

And yet, even with these new thoughts, Max was unprepared for the day when Flint finally left the shelter.

A family with two very noisy little girls wandered down the hall. They stopped in front of several cages housing small dogs.

Suddenly, "Hey Mom, come look! It's a pony! Can we get the pony, Mom? Dad? Can we, can we, can we?" shrieked one of the girls standing in front of Flint's kennel.

Flint rose to his feet and walked carefully toward the girl on the other side of the bars. He did, indeed, look almost like a pony beside the child. The second little girl clapped loudly with excitement, "She's right, it's a pony! You and Dad said they didn't have ponies in the shelter. But there's one right here. See, Mom?"

"Girls, that's a dog, not a pony, and he's way too big for our yard," responded their mother glancing briefly at Flint and then walking on.

The two sisters remained in front of Flint. One reached her sticky fingers through the bars and

Flint obligingly licked them.

"See? He likes us. Dad?" Their father drifted over to them and gazed at Flint thoughtfully. Flint wagged his tail.

"Honey, the sign here says he's an excellent guard dog and gentle with children. Our yard is small, but there's plenty of space for him to roam next door at the docks," he said, reaching through the bars to pet Flint.

The mother trailed back to look at Flint again. Tentatively, she patted Flint's muscular chest.

"Well, maybe."

And that was that. The two little girls shrieked with delight, and Flint had a new family and a home near a dock. It happened so quickly that there was no time for goodbyes. Max watched through his bars.

The last thing he heard was, "Do you think the pony will let us ride it?" and the outside door banged closed.

Flint's kennel sat empty. There was no familiar, massive head pressed in Max's direction. No more advice from across the hall. No more deep barks sending new kittens skittering for cover. Discouraged and lonely, Max curled up in the deepest shadows. Sometimes he closed his eyes on purpose. His ebony outline disappeared along the walls of the room. He went unnoticed. And then, late one afternoon, a visitor came unwittingly so close to Max that he stepped right on his paw. And that is when Maximus, the namesake of Roman gladiators, realized he had been born with a special skill: the skill of disappearing.

Days later, Max pressed himself tightly against a dark back wall and waited, eyes tightly shut. It was cleaning day. As usual, the shelter attendants picked up handfuls of kittens and carried them to a temporary cage. The elderly fisherman, Sven, helped with the transfer.

"I got 'em all out Dorothy," he yelled.

"Alright, go ahead and get it tidied up then," she called back.

Cold water began to pour along the floor, creeping over Max's paws. He forced perfect stillness, as it got wetter and deeper. Sven scrubbed the floor with a stout broom, soap foam spraying before him. Stiff bristles swept along Max's flank, but he stayed motionless. Finally, whistling loudly, the job done, Sven propped the door open and left. It was just as Max had planned. He waited another few minutes, shivering slightly, and then opened his eyes. Alone in the room, he looked at the open door. Black stealth, he slid into the hall. At the far end, he saw that the entrance door to the shelter stood ajar. A breeze whispered. Max flowed down the corridor past the kitten crowd who called out excitedly to him. No time for even a glance. He stepped at last, through that open door, into the freedom of a sunny afternoon.

THIRTEEN/THIRTEEN

"Hey Flint, what are we going to do today? Huh Flint? Huh? Flint?"

The question came from a speckled gray-and-white dog that circled rapidly around Flint as he spoke. Flint did not respond. Instead, he rolled lazily in the warm grass. His new family lived on a small street across from a busy harbor. An occasional car honked. Fishermen called to each other. Machines whirred and hoisted nets of chilled fish from boat to dock in the marina. Flint sighed with contentment.

"No little girls around all day, Flint. You said so yourself. Just us buddy. Hours of just us. Right? Right, Flint? Am I right?"

Flint trained one eye in the direction of the endless questions, but the speckled dog was moving so quickly that the next sentence came from a new direction.

"Halloo, Flint? Halloo?" called the zigzagging dog.

Flint suppressed a chuckle. This is how it always went with his new friend Hank. Constant talk. Constant motion. He rolled onto his back and wiggled side to side, paws in the air. The smell of crushed grass drifted out from under him. He remembered the cold cement of the shelter and sighed again, wagging his tail.

Finally, exasperated, Flint said, "Something wrong with your brain, boy? You need to stop moving!" He used his "scatter the kittens" voice from the shelter. It usually worked well with Hank.

"I'm an Australian Cattle Dog, Flint. You ever try to herd cattle in Australia? Huh, Flint? You can't stop moving. You gotta be fast or the cattle get away," said Hank. "You see this single black patch over my right eye? Why do I have the advantage over a dog with a patch over both eyes? Huh? Huh, Flint?"

Flint sat up slowly. He had heard all of this several times before but it looked like he was going to hear it all again. Hank's stream of chatter continued.

"Pretend you are a dumb bull. Just for a minute, okay Flint? Watch this Mr. Bull!" said Hank, and he leaned in close so that the black fur around his right eye filled Flint's field of view. And then Hank, with the patched eye fixed on the Rottweiler, began circling rapidly. He whirled faster and faster and then, suddenly, pivoted and began to move in the opposite direction. As always, Flint was impressed. He no longer saw a dog with a black eye patch. Now the dog who stared at him did so with his softer left eye, surrounded by pale, mottled fur.

Hank laughed out loud, "Uh-oh, Mr. Bull, this dog looks different than the other one. Is this the same dog? Could there be two dogs here or is it just one?" Switching directions in the circle yet again, he picked up speed.

"Confusing you Mr. Bull? Dogs with eye patches. Dogs with no patches. How many dogs are there? Maybe dozens!" shouted Hank as he raced

around Flint, wildly changing his direction again.

"Never stop moving. It's pure speed," said Hank triumphantly as he slid to a sudden stop.

Hank paused to take in a deep breath and Flint was ready. He wanted to change the subject.

"Things going any better with the chickens at your place?" he asked.

Hank looked a bit less sure of himself, "Yes, better. But I gotta stay busy. Gets real tempting watching those chickens. Trouble is, if you chase chickens all day, they get upset and won't lay eggs. Then there's trouble," finished Hank.

"We could go for an all-day patrol of the harbor? Get your mind off herding those chickens," suggested Flint.

And so, off they went. Bearish Flint marched along the street that paralleled the saltwater. Hank trailed at his flank, talking. Rounding a curve, they saw a huddle of dogs along the edge of the road, peering into a ditch. Hank picked up his pace.

"Do you see what I see Flint?" asked Hank. That's the Dalmatian twins. They're climbing into a *ditch!* They hate dirt, right Flint? How many times have they told us that dust disturbs their look? Huh? Flint?"

Flint had to agree. The Dalmatian twins, Torpedo and Nautilus definitely had an opinion about dirt of any kind. They spent most days licking, smoothing, and cleaning the islands of white fur that separated their black spots. The task was made all the more difficult by the fact that they lived at the marina's gas station. The clean beauty of their coats was a sharp contrast to the oil and grease around them.

"And look who else is up there, Flint. Do you see that? They've called in the military," Hank added. "Vader's with the twins. There must be something serious in that ditch."

With lazy power a German Shepherd turned in the direction of Hank's voice. Desert camouflage colored his beefy frame and sharp ears stood as he turned away from the excited Dalmatians in the ditch.

"Morning Vader," said Flint as they approached.

A nod from Vader. No words. He turned back to Nautilus and Torpedo in the trench below.

The twins were a confused salad of black spots. Tails wagged as they nudged something at their feet.

"Torpedo here! He's weak, Vader. Just lying in a pile of mud," one of them barked aloud.

The twins had an odd manner of speaking that took some getting used to. Perfectly identical at birth, even their mother struggled to tell them apart. As a result, all their comments started with a shout out of their own name. So deeply ingrained was this habit that it happened even when the two brothers were alone.

"Nautilus here!" shouted his brother. "He can't stand and he's way too filthy for us to pick up."

Vader growled and slid down into the ditch. With a gentle mouth, he picked something up and climbed back to the road.

Voice muffled by the bundle he carried, he said, "A runaway. No food."

The lump of fur stirred in Vader's jaws. "Just bugs really. Not much else for the last three days," it said.

Vader growled and slid down into the ditch.

Flint moved in for a closer look, startled. The cat he had tried so hard to befriend at the shelter, Max, hung like a limp sock from Vader's mouth.

"I know this cat. Name's Max. Last time I saw him he was behind bars at the shelter, locked up," said Flint.

"I closed my eyes, Flint. I disappeared," said Max.

Hank circled the group with concern. "He's eating bugs! We gotta get him food, right, Vader? Right, Flint?" He looked down at Nautilus and Torpedo who were still in the ditch.

"Nautilus here! YUCK!! Bugs are dirty and that cat eats them!"

"Torpedo here! I hate to tell you brother, but either one of your spots is moving or you got a big ugly bug on you right now!"

The two Dalmatians made a mad scramble out of the ditch. Once on the roadside, they began a dance of frantic scratching and shaking.

"Nautilus here! Is it gone Torpedo? Is it?" Nautilus shuddered. His brother looked him over from a safe distance.

"Torpedo here! We have an 'all clear' on the crawling bug, brother. Don't see it."

Flint and Hank watched the circus of spots, distracted. Vader still cradled a feeble Max in his jaws.

"13/13 is the best bet," he announced, his voice a thick mumble.

Flint nodded, and he, Hank, and Vader, headed toward the marina. Nautilus and Torpedo, disturbed by the bug encounter, elected not to come along. The main wooden dock split into multiple narrow fingers that extended out to the moored boats. These smaller walkways led to a wonderland of dropped food, remnants of fish, and other edible treasures. Metal doors blocked access to the walkways, and fishermen were careful to close and relock the doors as they came and went. But there was an exception, as every hungry dog or stray cat learned. It had always been true that inhabitants of one particular finger dock did not bother with security. Today, an empty crab pot wedged that steel door ajar. The animals slid unchallenged onto finger dock number 13.

Vader dropped Max onto the warm wood of the dock. The scent of fresh fish flowed from open boat hatches, hovered across decks and around drying nets. With a nudge from Vader, Max sat up.

"Okay. Got something for him," called Hank as he wrestled a portion of baitfish off the edge of a mooring rope. "This'll be tasty. Hey look! Also got two pieces of dropped salami. It's clean, not even stepped on," Hank said as he ran up and down the planks, nose to the ground.

As Flint and Vader watched, Max began to lick at a chunk of silvery fish.

"EAT! You need to eat faster," Hank urged Max who kept one eye on the food and one cautious eye on the bouncing Hank.

"Okay, found some gum here. Still got some taste in it," Hank said spitting a large purple blob onto the rising pile of scraps in front of Max. "You eat so slow! No wonder you're weak. You should . . ."

"SIT DOWN, Hank," roared Flint. " Do you know what irony is? Irony is when you scare a poor starving cat with a . . . PILE OF FOOD! Max might rather eat bugs, in peace and quiet!"

Hank sat abruptly, tail still wagging. 'Here we go. Another outburst,' he thought, shaking his head with sympathy. 'Poor Flint got born with muscles but not enough speed. Who wouldn't get upset if they had to live their whole life in the slow lane?'

"Sure thing, Flint," Hank said tail thumping. "I'll just sit here 'till the little fella eats all of it. Except for the gum. I can put the gum back. Sound good? Huh, Flint?"

Vader interrupted, "As a military dog in the armed forces, sometimes I had to go days without eating. Take your time Max. There will be food tomorrow."

Before Vader, Hank, and Flint left, they guided Max to a bright red boat called *Ladybug*. It was moored snugly in slip 13. No sign of the fisherman who owned it. Everything was quiet.

"This is boat slip 13 on dock 13. 13/13. No guarantees, but it's the best bet on the dock for safe shelter. You need a place for the night," said Vader.

"Hope he takes you. Could be complicated though," said Flint. He seemed worried as he watched Max climb aboard and under an old hammock.

"Am I crazy? Why is an unlucky black cat climbing aboard a boat whose address is not one but *two* unlucky numbers?" Max wondered aloud, overwhelmed with exhaustion. Vader, Hank, and Flint were already halfway down the dock and did not respond. Max curled up and fell asleep in the sun, stomach full.

He startled awake. Hours had passed with the sun now much lower on the horizon. A menacing shadow covered him. An old man in a thick wool sweater stood within grabbing distance.

A sharp inhalation of surprise, and then, "Maximus! Namesake of Roman gladiators *and* an escaped prisoner? How did you come to be aboard the *Ladybug?*" the voice asked.

To his horror, Max recognized Sven, the old man from the shelter. After all of this, he was going right back to the cement kitten cage. Anger flared as he realized that Flint had known who owned this boat. But slowly as the fisherman spoke, the meaning of his words filtered through to Max.

"Almost lost my job over you Maximus. To be honest, I'm glad you escaped. No family was gonna adopt you anyway," said the old man. Max listened, keeping a stiff distance.

"Perhaps you'll consider staying aboard the *Ladybug*? Here at 13/13, I've got no room for nonsense superstition," he said moving to stroke Max.

Max stepped out of reach.

"Don't mind a little attitude either," Sven said, chuckling. He ambled off, leaving Max to settle back under the faded hammock.

And so Max stayed, just as Flint had hoped he would. Life flowed at 13/13. Max rolled out of a pile of nets, just as the fishing boats returned loaded with their morning catch. Sven rarely took his boat out of the harbor anymore, and that suited Max just fine. When the sea-going vessels arrived, the hatches were thrown open and the catch was exposed, spilling onto the deck and sometimes back into the water. Raucous groups of gulls tipped Max off to the best opportunities. As a load of fish was lifted up, morsels plummeted downward. Max, a shadow in the shadows, waited. Invariably, a sharp beak skirmish broke out among the gulls. Taking advantage of the chaos, he selected a target. Running fast, belly low to the deck, he swallowed the fish before the birds realized he was among them. More than once the gulls bruised him with a sharp peck. Sliding with hungry joy on the wet deck, protecting his eyes from the feathered mob, he ate his fill. The food bowl that Sven dependably put out each day, went untouched. Where was the challenge in tame food? Contentment filled his heart. Afternoon winds whispered seaweed around his bed of nets. At last, he had a home, a human protector, and food. Flint came often to visit but Max remained aloof. Why, he asked himself, should he bother with friendship? The "creepy" black cat had everything he needed. And that is how a full year of days slid past. Max lived alone because he preferred it that way.

*Why, the black cat asked himself,
should he bother with friendship?*

TANGLED ROOTS

The arrival changed everything. A wind blew into the harbor as sunset approached. The air sang in color. Max gazed west. A bright splash moved on the ocean, separating itself from the horizon and the lowering sun. A mirage of cherry, orange, and black, it appeared and disappeared from sight, sailing against the sky. At first, Max saw only a single, small wooden boat with a very unusual sail. But on closer inspection, there were actually two boats. Traditional white sails powered a sailing sloop, which towed the smaller boat. The follower trailed on a line, sail full, so far behind the larger vessel, that it seemed independent. Max squinted to focus on the spot of color that was the petite boat's sail. A masked warrior amid cherry blossoms painted the canvas. A red dog sat, alone, beneath that sail, looking for all the world as if he actually piloted the boat. He gazed toward the harbor, and it seemed, straight at Max.

Darkness settled as the duo of boats entered the harbor. Men's voices carried in the evening air. The newcomers arrived and registered. Somehow, Max knew what would happen even before it came to pass. And so, he was not surprised when the visitors were assigned to the open boat slip next to 13/13. Noise and shouted instructions continued as the large sloop moored and the small sailing dingy snuggled up close behind it. A man with a heavy limp and a faded coast guard jacket hailed *Ladybug.*

"Evening neighbor," he called to Sven who was relaxing in his green hammock.

"Welcome to you! Making a home here on dock 13 or just sailing through?" asked Sven.

Max strained to see next door in the gloom. The vivid sail on the smaller boat was furled. No opportunity for a closer look at the warrior painting. No sign of the red dog. The tiny vessel rocked behind its larger parent boat. Moonlight reflected off the dingy name: *Ninja*.

"Relieved to make port at last. Long journey. Name's Kegun. Kegun Hatsukami. Everyone calls me 'Cap'. Been transferred to the coast guard here."

"That sail on your dingy, kinda unusual around here," said Sven.

"True enough," said Cap, giving a friendly nod. With no further explanation he headed belowdecks for the evening.

The next morning Max woke to murmurs from next door. Dawn light bounced off the water, dock, and boats. The red dog, alone in the dingy, bent toward the rising sun and spoke.

"I am a sentry at our planet's gate. I watch and wait. With a soldier's heart, I pledge to protect the unprotected."

Curious, Max watched. The dog turned slowly into the cat's penetrating stare. Max started. The dog's gaze suggested Egypt, ancient Egypt. Although he stood on an ordinary wooden boat, he carried himself like royalty. His almond eyes looked as if someone had traced a thick black crayon around each of them. Wrapped in a red coat, cream fur trimmed his flanks. An impossible curl bent his tail.

"Name's Charlie," said the exotic creature.

"Max. Met a lot of dogs. Never seen a dog like you," said Max.

"Shiba. I'm a Shiba Inu. Ancestors from ancient Japan," responded the red dog, gaze unwavering. "Arrived last night. I'm going for a look around this morning. Like to come along?"

But Max being Max was not looking for a friend. "No thanks," he said. And that was his response for many months. Left behind in solitude, he watched as Charlie moved with purpose, straight into the lives of the harbor inhabitants.

Right next door, Max observed rare magic. Hank began visiting Charlie. He often arrived at twilight with his typical frenetic bounce and rapid-fire speech. Charlie would lie, front paws crossed, attentive but quiet. One evening Max overheard an exchange.

"Hank?" Charlie said when Hank was taking a

Charlie's arrival changed everything.

quick inhale between stories.

"Yah? Yah, Charlie? Yah?" said Hank.

"Talking or not talking, fast or slow, my friend, I like you just the same," said Charlie.

Hank did not respond or even seem to notice Charlie's comment. But oddly, the tempo of Hank's visits began to shift. Hank himself changed. Sometimes, he would be the familiar Hank, bouncing and talking and throwing words like snowballs. But sometimes, after an hour, Hank's speech would slow. He would wag his tail. A different dog showed up. Unbelievably, he would sit, tail slowly thumping. No speech. Sitting peacefully as night closed in.

Not long after his arrival, Charlie strolled by Flint's front yard. It was a typical day for Flint. His little girls focused on their favorite game. The Rottweiler carried a toy saddle with a teddy bear rider, on his broad back.

"Go, go, giddy up pony," squealed one of his girls, an ice-cream cone dripping on her hand.

"Time to gallop!" laughed the other, clutching a

half-eaten cookie. Charlie slowed to watch.

Flint called out amid the noise, "Charlie, right? Hank says you docked in the harbor a few weeks ago. Hear you've got a strange sail on your dingy?"

Charlie nodded, "Yep. Charlie. Transferred by the coast guard."

Flint absent-mindedly licked the hand of the little girl who dripped ice cream and tried again, "What about the masked warrior on your sail and that other painted stuff? What does it mean?"

"That figure is a ghost of Cap's ancestors. It's a reminder that he and his father and his father's father, all the way back to his great-grandfather's great-great-grandfather, were warriors," said Charlie.

Flint interrupted, "Keep talking but speed up. Gotta move to keep the girls happy." He broke into a light trot, the teddy bear rider bouncing. "Sorry. Did you say that's a ghost soldier painted on your sail?"

Charlie moved to stay alongside Flint. "You've heard of the Samurai? Or perhaps the Ninja?"

"Sure, I've heard of them," said Flint looking at

Charlie, "Don't see why that matters though? The Samurai are long gone. The last of those warriors walked the planet centuries ago."

"Ah, but Cap and I see it differently. We believe that the Ninja and the Samurai live on, in the present. They *are* Cap and Cap is them." And then, he added under his breath, "and so also for the Shiba Inu. My ancestors are me and, I am them."

"Can't say I know much about the Shiba Inu," Flint said.

In response, Charlie began a story. He related the legend of the Shiba Inu who, in ancient times, protected the Palace of the Sun. Man depended on fierce watchdogs for survival. The feudal Samurai and Ninja respected the Shiba Inu for their grit and loyalty. As the world modernized, however, stories of the exploits of these warrior dogs were buried in time.

Flint listened, nodding.

A loud screech abruptly interrupted all conversation.

"Oh no! LOOOOK! He fell backwards. Hit his

heeeead," screamed the little cookie-eater.

Indeed, the teddy bear was down. Not only down but hideously down. He lay flat on his face, dragging behind Flint, arms outstretched as if begging for rescue. The tape that had, moments ago, attached him to the saddle was snarled full of grass, twigs and a few small ants.

"Unusual day for you?" asked Charlie. He had to raise his voice to be heard above the uproar because now both sisters sobbed loudly and their mother had jumped up off the front porch swing in alarm.

Charlie got no response from Flint who had already turned to his crying charges. This was not the first time the game of "Pony" had gone wrong. Expertly Flint lifted the teddy off the ground and rubbed him vigorously against his flank. Dirt, grass and ants flew everywhere. He carried the bear, much cleaner, face up, to the ice-cream-cone girl. She stopped crying. Licking first one childish face and then the other, tail wagging, he restored order with astonishing efficiency. Smiling, their mother turned back to the porch swing.

"Days can be a bit crazy here, but I love this family. I waited so long at that shelter," Flint said.

Charlie nodded. "Yes, I can see. Might be hard to get away though, with all this responsibility. Maybe I could come join you now and then?"

From that day forward, Charlie showed up frequently. The front yard routine became even livelier. The children tied bells and flowers to collars, rigged up wagons to pull, and built secret forts to guard. "Red Dog and Pony" became the new favorite game. A bond tightened between Charlie and Flint.

Charlie met two Labradors in the early days after his arrival. Sugar was the golden one, and her chocolate companion was Drucker. Light and dark, they travelled together. Sugar's bright fur lit up the harbor, even on a cloudy day. Drucker, with a coat the color of shadows, rarely left her side. They arrived, most days, at a beach across from where Charlie's boat was moored. Relaxing in his dingy, Charlie observed that the Labs were accomplished waterdogs, surfers in fact. They attended a man who crossed the sand in a motorized wheelchair.

"His legs don't work. But always, he's yearned to be a surfer," Drucker explained to Charlie. "When he discovered canine surfing he came a step closer to his dream. Sugar and I learned to surf, even though he couldn't."

The man and his two dogs, Drucker and Sugar, traveled along the coast, entering surfing contests. They won often. The dogs lived for the ocean and for surfing big waves in particular.

Sugar and Drucker became a familiar sight for Charlie. He relaxed in his small boat and enjoyed their antics on many a lazy afternoon. Fur streaming saltwater, they bounced in the surf. As time passed, Charlie began to observe something else. Folks who visited the beach regularly "forgot" Styrofoam bowls, metal cans, or cigarette butts. Some would even leave the most dangerous of trash, the closed plastic rings that encircle cans of soda. The man in the wheelchair saw the offenders but never confronted them. Instead, while the Labradors enjoyed the surf, he spent his time quietly picking up trash. Sometimes, at the end of the day, he would send the two dogs on patrol to pick up the bottles or papers that he could not reach by wheelchair.

One drowsy afternoon, a regular group of beachgoers got up and left. They carried their blankets and food but left behind a plastic fork, an aluminum can, and a clump of closed plastic rings. They straggled laughing toward their car. The man wheeled toward the set of rings, half-buried in the sand. He struggled to pick them up but could not quite reach them.

He shouted to the departing group, "Hey you! Come back and get your trash!"

Charlie looked up from his boat, surprised. He had never seen the man challenge even the worst offender. One of the group stopped abruptly and turned. A grinning skull tattoo slid along the oiled muscles of his chest. His face twisted with annoyance as he walked back toward the wheelchair. Drucker and Sugar surfed in the distance.

"Don't you be telling us what to do mister," he said.

"I'm sick and tired of watching you and your friends litter, buddy. At least pick up the plastic rings. Do you know what happens to creatures if those get in the ocean?" he said, shifting in his wheelchair.

Tattoo man leaned down threateningly, "So what if a few birds get a plastic noose around their necks? What do I care? Mind your own business or there's gonna be trouble."

Charlie slowly stood up in his sailboat. His dingy floated a distance away but he could see and hear everything.

"Littering is against the law. Police might want to know you guys litter here all the time," persisted the man in the wheelchair.

Tattoo man's arm snaked out violently. Charlie started barking before contact was made. The furious sound startled the entire beach. The man in the wheelchair had time to pull back from that muscular fist. Heads on the beach turned as people became aware of what was happening. Several jumped up in alarm. Drucker and Sugar turned toward the commotion and splashed out of the water.

"Leave that man alone or I'm calling the police now!" yelled one of the beach-goers.

A woman under a nearby umbrella shouted, "It's disgusting that you leave your garbage for others to clean up. You're messing up our beach."

And, "I want that dog over there to stop barking and it seems he's barking at *you*," said another. "Clean it up and get lost!'

Dripping seawater, Drucker and Sugar moved close, hugging the wheelchair.

Tattoo man was not stupid. He backed off. Kicking his trash along the sand, he stomped away.

And so, a pact was formed. If a beach-goer "forgot" to take their trash, the man in the wheelchair could be counted on to ask them to pick it up. He was always polite. The man learned that he had backup even when Drucker and Sugar were surfing. If anyone threatened him, the red dog relaxing in a nearby boat could be counted on to sound an alarm. Once alerted, the Labradors and the regular beach-goers came to his aid. Sugar and

Drucker no longer needed to clean up the beach at the end of the day. The sand was already clean.

Early after his arrival in the harbor, Charlie dropped in to meet the Dalmatian twins. There had been an accident at the gas station. A pool of oil had reached out and tripped Nautilus. In mere seconds, foul grease smothered his pristine fur. Frantic, he licked and cleaned. Torpedo tried to help but it was useless. Oil clung like black glue to his coat. He did not recognize himself. Deeply sad, he lay down and refused to get up.

That first morning, as Charlie approached the gas station, Torpedo came out to meet him, anxious.

"Torpedo here. Not a good time. No visitors. Nautilus can't get up. Oil. Can't fix him. No visitors today," he said, turning back to his brother.

"Name's Charlie. Sailed in not long ago. I know a thing or two about oil. Perhaps I could sit with both of you for awhile?" he responded.

Torpedo accepted that first offer with hesitation but from then on he eagerly awaited Charlie's arrival. Charlie told the brothers what he knew about oil on feathers and fur. In his travels, he had witnessed ocean spills and the devastation it caused. He reassured the brothers that in the case of fur, time was the cure. Charlie visited regularly. He sat without words, absorbing a daily dose of Nautilus's misery. He listened but offered no advice. Weeks passed. As Charlie had predicted, the matted fur loosened and began to fall out. One morning Nautilus made a small joke about his knotted fur. He laughed. He got up and walked around the gas station again. Hope returned long before the last of the oil-soaked coat dropped away. When Nautilus finally felt confident enough to venture out of the gas station and back into the world, it was unclear which of the Dalmatian brothers felt greater loyalty toward Charlie.

Max watched as the roots of Charlie's life slowly became all tangled up with the roots of other lives. As for Max, nothing changed. He had no desire to get close to anyone.

One warm evening, just like so many others, Max boarded a nearby fishing vessel. The

*Charlie's life slowly became
all tangled up with the
roots of other lives.*

squawking gulls and the promise of fresh fish lured him. He dove joyously for a delicious morsel, as he had thousands of times before. This time, he slipped unexpectedly on the wet deck. Unable to control his speed he plummeted, out of control, through the hatch and down the ladder into darkness. Hitting his head hard on the way down, he landed stunned in the refrigerated hold of the boat. Up on deck, a fisherman whistled as he completed the last of his day's work: a big load of fish caught and now loaded onto the dock. Time to lock everything down. It was Friday. A full weekend out of town beckoned. He strolled to the hatch door and, as was his habit, glanced downward. Seeing nothing, he closed the hatch. Below in the hold, a black cat lay on a black floor.

COLD

Chilled water sloshed and gurgled. Not a speck of light disturbed the darkness. Max struggled back into consciousness.

"So wet," he thought shivering. "Can't see anything."

And then he remembered. He had fallen. He was deep beneath the deck of a fishing boat. And somehow the hatch was sealed. Blinking his eyes against the weight of blackness, Max stepped toward where he thought the ladder should be. He crashed painfully into something metal, stumbling sideways into a pool of frigid water. His head throbbed and he was oddly thirsty. Leaning down he licked at the pool of water he stood in.

"Blah! Salt!"

Max shivered again, wet fur plastered to his

body. A cooling unit hummed somewhere nearby, dropping the temperature of the hold for the next catch.

"The next catch!" Max thought. It was the weekend. Another catch would not be dropping down into the hold for several days.

But someone would look for him, surely? They would notice he was missing by dinnertime, wouldn't they? Realization dawned slowly. Of course no one would be looking for him. He came and went as he pleased. He did not bother with friends. Even Sven had accepted his standoffishness. Max had preferred it that way.

He felt his aloneness grow. Alarm squeezed his heart. He had nobody, just as he had insisted. And now, he felt so lonely and afraid that he could hardly breathe. Lost, deep down in that dark refrigerator, he would be without food. His cold fur dripped and he licked himself.

"Aghh. Salt again."

Max shook violently as ice crystallized on his fur. Alarm turned to panic. Food and water would not matter. The cold was going to kill him first.

"HELP! SOMEBODY! PLEASE! DOWN HERE!"

Max yelled for an hour, but there was no answer to his calls. At first, he warmed slightly with the effort and the fear. But eventually his voice tired and became hoarse. Hopeless, he realized that he was going to freeze to death.

Hours and hours passed. Max became so cold that his legs stiffened and he could no longer move or call. He knew that once his body temperature got dangerously low, he would begin to feel sleepy. He gave up and let his mind drift, eyes closed now. Confused memories floated in his thoughts. He pictured his brothers and sisters playing like happy butterflies. But something was wrong. The tumbling kittens were barking. That made no sense. His mind slid away from his siblings and touched on Sven and the scent of his woolen sweater. Sven turned to Max, and then, he too began barking. Max was so cold now that he did not try to understand this craziness. He could

*Max shook violently as ice
crystallized on his fur.*

feel sleep rolling toward him. It felt warmer. He just wanted to give up and sleep. But the barking would not let him float away.

"Make that barking stop," he whispered.

And then a loud angry human voice filtered down into the hold.

"Stop barking! I gotta get to sleep," yelled a woman's voice. "Get away from the hatch you crazy red dog. GET!"

"Yeah, I gotta sleep too," thought Max, so drowsy from the cold. He curled further into himself.

The barking did not even slow. Now, to make matters worse, deep scratching sandpapered the wood over Max's head. Loud human curses mingled with the other sounds.

"I'll shut him up with the hose!" yelled a man's voice.

And then, there was the sound of water. High-pressure water. It thundered on the deck above Max's head. So much water that it leaked down through the hatch and dripped onto Max. More misery. Max pulled further into a ball to avoid the drops. The barking stopped.

At last, Max could drift toward sleep. All was quiet.

It may have been an hour or it may have been less. Max had no idea really, down in that icy cave. What he did know was that he was jolted abruptly out of his stupor. If a single barker had been irritating, what he now heard was a traffic jam of noise. Multiple barking dogs howled directly above where Max lay. Somehow, something felt familiar and pictures appeared at the edge of his consciousness. A sail painted with a warrior, and barking, a brown bear with barking, surfboards with barking, salt-and-pepper spots with more barking. So much barking!

And then, light! The hatch flew open. Warm air tumbled down the ladder toward Max.

"Must be something down here. Never run across any dog would brave another water hosing *and* bring friends," a voice grumbled.

"Maybe there's a rat but I don't know how anything could survive the cold," said another voice, footsteps descending.

There was a low whistle and Max felt himself being lifted up.

"Hard to believe but there's a cat down here. Froze solid, looks like. Don't think it's alive," said the whistler.

Max felt himself being laid out on the deck above. The hatch banged shut.

"I'm alive!" he wanted to shout. But he could not even blink his eyes.

"Hey, look at that. Now that this little fella's up here, the dogs are leaving. Never saw a stranger thing, so much commotion over a lost cat," murmured a woman close to Max's ear.

"Nope. He didn't make it, poor little guy. Probably best to leave him right here tonight. Find out tomorrow morning who lost a cat."

With that, Max heard the humans departing. He sprawled on the planks of the deck encased in his stiffly frozen fur. Still cold. Still alone.

"I've got you, Max. I've got you," said a voice. A strong tongue began licking his fur, melting the ice.

Warmth crept in.

"I've got you, my friend. I've got you, Max," a voice, Charlie's voice, repeated over and over. He curled close to Max. His body radiated heat. Max wanted to huddle closer.

"Max, I'm going to be your friend until you are *my* friend," said Charlie.

And so, Charlie saved Max's life and everyone on the dock knew it. Sure the other dogs had helped. But it was Charlie who noticed that Max was not aboard Sven's boat that night, and Charlie took action. He followed Max's scent along the dock until the trail ended at a closed hatch on an empty fishing boat. By the time Charlie stood above him, Max could no longer call up from the hold. Charlie raised the alarm. The only response he got was a drenching with high-pressure water. So he changed the plan. Bruised and soaking wet, he ran along the dock, calling for the support of others. Flint, Hank, Torpedo, Nautilus, Sugar, Drucker, and even Vader dropped what they were doing. Braving a punishing hose, they gathered on that boat and sounded the alarm with Charlie. Powerful together, their numbers changed everything. Max escaped death that night.

Everyone saw the change. Fierce feelings of gratitude and loyalty filled Max's heart. He no longer focused just on food, water, shelter and himself. Charlie's steady presence, and the rescue, had changed the black cat's narrow existence. Charlie opened a larger world for Max. With time, Max would come to learn that this new, larger life brought joy, but it could also bring pain.

BLOOD

Fear stalks dogs just as it haunts people. Nightmares crawl into the daylight and refuse to depart. For hours Charlie had been lost in his head. Again. Angry shouting exploded from his past. A snarling growl vibrated in his throat. Adrenaline surged.

"Get the cables on! Pull tighter! Brace yourselves. We're going overboard with those monsters!"

High-pitched calls of distress pulled at him. Frightened. Blood on the water, blood in the boat, blood on him. So much blood. Powerless.

Silence. The stillness slowly roused Charlie. His sailboat home rocked rhythmically. The fear, the noise, and the luminous dark eyes leaked away. Charlie shook his tense muscles and stood up. He climbed from belowdecks and up into the light of

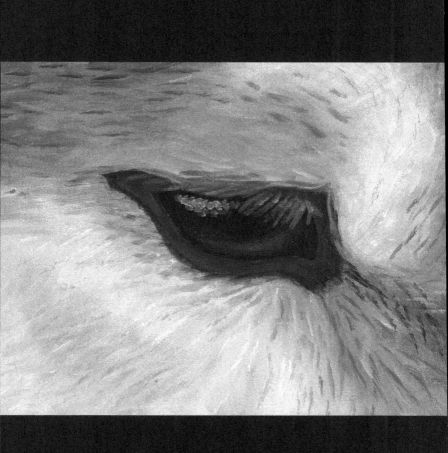

*Fear stalks dogs just
as it haunts people.*

his tropical harbor. As he did every dawn, Charlie repeated the same ritual. He bent toward the eastern horizon and the rising sun.

"I am a sentry at our planet's gate. I wait and watch. With a soldier's heart, I pledge to protect the unprotected."

On this particular morning, Charlie inhaled deeply the scents of his home harbor. As skilled as ten fingers and a camera, his nose zoomed and touched and remembered. Colorful smells rushed at him: salty water, frying bacon, boat diesel, and the scent of his friend Max, next door. And there were other smells, which were deeper and shyer. Charlie's nose hinted at barnacle-studded piers, slippery fish scales, and warm mud.

Turning his head and stretching, he spied Max, ambling sleepily down the dock. He leaped onto the boat deck next to Charlie.

"It's not noon yet. You sick?" asked Charlie.

"Believe me, I know it's early. Any time I catch your secret chanting and bowing, I know it's way too soon to be awake," Max said, licking a paw and sweeping it over his face.

"Max, my friend, you and I have talked about this: it's not secret and it's not chanting," said Charlie, "It's something I do to remind myself about a pledge I made, years ago."

"Yes, I know. But what happened back then? Why won't you share the story with me?" interrupted Max. Then more gently he encouraged, "I know you have nightmares. I understand that something haunts you. Talk to me."

As he had many other times before, Charlie just shook his head and changed the subject.

"The poachers struck again last night. Heard anything about it?" he asked.

Max sighed with frustration and then allowed the conversation to flow in another direction.

"That's exactly why I'm here so early. Overheard some fishermen talking. Raids happening south of us. Pretty successful too. So far the coast guard hasn't been able to stop them," he said, his tail twitching angrily.

"I know what you're thinking Max. I share

your worry," said Charlie. "They're predators but we must bide our time. That's all we can do at this point."

"Let them dare to come further north!" Max hissed.

The discussion continued as the horizon brightened, but ultimately Max respected Charlie's input on the matter of the poachers. The two friends spent the remainder of that morning warming in the sun, with no further discussion of Charlie's past.

SIRENS

Too late. Sirens funneled down the dirt road but found only tire tracks where the poachers had been. Coast guard lights flashed from the sea, illuminating a quiet beach littered with empty turtle nests and pieces of broken eggshell. First on the scene, Captain Kegun Hatsukami stepped a weary boot out of his truck. A single green turtle hatchling flip-flopped in the headlights. Crossing the sand with his signature limp, Cap studied the scene and read the story.

"They didn't have a chance, Joe. Not a chance. Must be dozens of baby turtles broke out of their shells tonight, only to be stolen. We're too late. Always too late," said Cap, his voice rising in anger.

"You can't blame yourself, Cap," said his partner Joe, coming to stand by his side. "This is a professional poaching ring. They learn about their target animal. It's big money and criminals that drive poaching," he said with disgust.

Cap kicked the sand. "These turtles are an endangered species, Joe. If we can't protect them then we just aren't doing our job. Period!" He climbed back into the coast guard truck and slammed the door hard.

Joe stood a while longer, alone on the beach. He looked up at the full moon, spat into the sand, and walked back to the truck.

Further south, under the same moon, a dented white Dodge pickup raced along the coastal road. Triumphant shouting and laughter drifted through the open windows.

"We did it, boys! We did it again," boomed Nitro, the driver, as he expertly swerved around a pothole. An explosion of dark hair covered his head, face, and chin.

"Yeah but . . . but Nitro, that was just too close. We could hear the sirens," whined a man wedged against the passenger door. Squeaky, as he'd been called since he was a kid, slouched in his signature red sweatshirt. As usual, he kept his head tucked under the wide hood, face in shadow. When Nitro did not respond he pulled deeper into his red tent until his high-pitched complaining became unintelligible.

"You've got to RELAX, Squeaky, and realize we aren't going to get caught. We're too smart for the coast guard," laughed the third poacher. A fat purple scar wandered along his cheek, passed his right eye, and disappeared under a gray nylon skullcap. He sat, squeezed in the middle seat of the cab.

"You gotta put your trust in ol' Tex here," he continued with a drawl. I've studied the habits of the green turtles and I'm an expert, which is more than I can say for the local coast guard! You just let Nitro and me handle this. Wow. What a night! Nitro, hey . . . what do you think the haul is worth this time? How much money you think we're gonna get . . . huh?"

The gravelly reply from Nitro disappeared

*A fat purple scar wandered along
his cheek and disappeared under
a gray nylon skullcap.*

out the window and the three poachers began laughing again. In the back of the pickup, the stolen baby turtles bounced inside their cages. The truck picked up speed.

A CAGE WITHIN A CAGE

The motorcycle roared like a jet, shaking everyone from their morning sleep. Lava, the Bulldog, descended daintily from her perch in the sidecar. Her arrival was a weekly ritual on the dock. With practiced ease, she pushed her head against a foreleg, easing her thick riding goggles up.

Lava was somewhat of a legend. She described herself as a "washed up" show dog. But that was the modest version of the story. Basically, Lava had walked out on fame. Years of her youth passed as she honed the skills of a competitive show dog. She paraded, trotted, and obeyed in the ring. To hear her tell the story, she longed for adventure when all the while she was being brushed and manicured. Her family was not a family at all. As part of a large group of dogs, she was a treasured object to be

*The motorcycle
roared like a jet.*

groomed for fame and recognition.

One evening, she found herself standing near an open door, collar loose, leash insecure. Without hesitation, she walked out. Looking up and down the busy sidewalk, she panicked for just a moment. What was she doing? And then she saw it. Parked along the curb, a large motorcycle with a sidecar. She climbed in and crouched low in the dusk. Less than an hour passed before the owner hopped on his bike and pulled into the traffic. When he glanced over and saw that a bulldog was riding alongside him, he swerved violently. Fortunately, he avoided a crash. Lava wagged her tail and turned on her best showgirl smile.

To give the man credit, he did pull over and search for a way to return her, but there was nothing. She had slipped her head out of that sloppily applied collar. Collar and leash fell to the floor as she left. Lava was a mystery, a lost dog. Luckily for her, the biker moved to a new city soon after, and he kept moving. Their meeting was pure chance but the man adored her. And so, Lava settled blissfully into a strange new life.

On this particular harbor visit, Lava sought out Vader and spoke urgently to him.

"I want some action, Vader. I just can't keep passing by. Something has to be done!" said Lava.

She reminded him that, on her recent trips to the marina, the motorcycle passed a pathetic sight. Blinding heat or pouring rain, it never changed. A dog sat alone, sometimes without food, in a small cage. The cage was so small that he could barely walk. The cage sat in a yard, surrounded by a tall metal penitentiary fence. As Lava described it, he sat locked in a "cage within a cage". This was not the first time Lava had appealed to Vader. As the senior dog on the dock, he assumed leadership in these matters. Lava had lobbied multiple times on behalf of the imprisoned dog.

"And now I've learned that his people are moving. They'll pack him up like he's a shovel or a lawnmower. They don't care, Vader. If we don't do something soon, we'll lose our chance to help him," said Lava.

Vader responded with few words, as was his habit, "There are terrible injustices in this world Lava. Some of them can't be changed."

"But Vader! This is a dog problem. Solitary confinement forever . . . " begged Lava.

"No Lava. It's a human problem. We dogs have no power there. As sorry as I feel for the prisoner, my decision is final."

By now Max and several dogs had gathered, listening.

A voice spoke.

"When the goodhearted are silent, evil grows stronger."

Heads turned, recognizing Charlie's voice. Vader had long been the commander on the dock. Charlie spoke with respect but he gazed directly at the German Shepherd. The dogs waited.

"I cannot encourage interference in the world of men," said Vader.

"I respect your opinion Vader, but I stand with Lava," said Charlie.

Max slid between Charlie and Vader, a feline buffer.

"Dog's name is Rocky. Sometimes he's low on food, so he's always grateful for scraps." As a habitual roamer, Max had passed the "cage within a cage" many times. If there was going to be a call to action, he had weeks of reconnaissance to offer.

Tension eased. As for Vader, he remained aloof. A hesitant discussion began about the possible liberation of Rocky. Max offered a wealth of information. He explained to the listening animals that the prison yard was bordered on one side by a narrow alley. People filled the alley during the day, but at night, quiet reigned.

"There's more," said Max, "Dog's got a generous heart. Said his people just don't think about him anymore. Young couple. New baby, then another one. No time for a Redbone Hound out in the back yard."

A shiver went through the assembled dogs.

"But Lava, if he's free, he won't have a home. Right, Flint? Right?" asked Hank.

"My biker sees Rocky when we drive past. There's room in our sidecar for another dog," said Lava.

"Good to know, Lava. If we can get him out of there, he'll have a place to go," said Charlie. "I suggest we form a squad. Volunteers?"

Lava, Max, and Flint stepped forward. Others followed. Vader stood silent. The other dogs knew better than to ask about his decision.

Finally, Vader spoke up, "Moonless nights are best."

And so, on the next dark night, the entire group trotted out of the harbor, Charlie at the head. Taking the rear, Vader slid in and out of the shadows. Max traveled alone.

They arrived along the fence bordering the alley. Deserted. Rocky stirred in his prison.

"Is someone out there?" he asked, his ears pricking up.

"It's me, Lava, the motorcycle dog. We've come to get you out of there," Lava whispered.

"Be careful. If the people in that house hear you . . . I don't know," he said shaking his head. He rose to his feet, nose to the wire.

No dog responded. They were too busy. Muted instructions from Charlie drifted in the night air. Working as a team, they began digging. When one dog tired, another took its place. Piles of dirt mounded up in the alley. As they dug, two tunnels pushed under the fence and toward the open yard. Rocky blinked his eyes uncertainly. He was taken aback at the speed and efficiency of the action. Both tunnels burst open simultaneously. Dogs shot out: two muddy Labradors, a panting Cattle dog, twin Dalmatians, a Rottweiler, and a tense German Shepherd. As one, they turned to watch the last dog step through the tunnel.

"Excellent," said Charlie, "Okay Flint, give it some muscle. I need you inside that second cage before someone hears us. The rest of you, on guard."

Flint hunched his shoulders at the edge of Rocky's enclosure. Dirt flew. At one point he paused, panting, and Vader stepped in to work while he rested. The Rottweiler pushed his head through the last bit of dirt and rock, into the smaller cage.

*Working as a team,
they began digging.*

"Let's go, Rocky," he said, breathing hard, then disappeared into the passage.

Rocky followed and stepped out onto the grass. Free at last! Delirious with excitement he let loose a Redbone's hunting howl.

The rescue squad froze instantly. All heads turned toward the dark house. Sheepish, Rocky quieted.

Then, "Uh-oh, lights going on!" warned Drucker.

"Hoped to avoid this," said Charlie, "You all know what to do."

"Here they come," called Sugar as a door banged open.

Bright lights flooded the yard. A young man in white socks came off the porch at a run, shouting and clapping, "WHAT in tarnation! How'd you all get in here?"

At Charlie's signal, the dogs moved as one animal. Surrounding Rocky, they maneuvered him into their midst. Rocky streamed along, like a buffalo in a herd, heading for the outside fence. He shot through the outer tunnel and into the alley followed closely by Flint, Sugar, and Drucker. Instructions to "get the prisoner out first" accomplished.

"Delilah, get me the bear spray, NOW!" roared the man.

"Bear spray? Really?" said a woman's voice, "You forget to feed that dog half the time. Who cares if it runs away?"

"Cuz it's *my* dog! My dog! I will not let a bunch of strays steal my property," he said running back to the porch and grabbing a silver canister from his wife. Somewhere inside the house, a baby cried.

"Now look, you woke the baby!" She disappeared into the house.

Aiming the canister, the man ran forward, "This spray will halt a charging grizzly bear. Let's see what it does to dogs."

The rescuers milled and stampeded, making it difficult to single out any particular animal. No easy target. Herd strategy. At first, everything flowed, just exactly as Charlie had envisioned. The man sprayed wildly into the night air, but with little effect, as dog after dog disappeared under the fence. As he advanced, the man stumbled forward into a chemical mist of his own making. His eyes watered, he coughed and his rage increased.

Lava wriggled into one of the passageways, Charlie waiting behind her. Torpedo crawled into the other tunnel with Vader crouching, ready to crawl in next. Charlie's tunnel opened. Clear to go. Then it happened.

"Torpedo sees a beetle in the tunnel," came Max's voice from the alley, "He's stuck."

"Move it Torpedo!" growled Vader. But Torpedo had come to a dead stop in the tunnel.

"Torpedo here. If I touch it, it's gonna crawl on me," came a panicked voice from the tunnel.

Distracted by the backup in the tunnel, Vader did not see the canister being aimed, close range, at his eyes. Charlie took it all in. In keeping with an ancient warrior code, he turned back toward Vader. Without thought, he launched himself toward the threat. The man turned and fired. The spray cloud enveloped Charlie. His throat and lungs burned.

He wheezed and gasped. Eyes forced shut, blind; he sagged to the ground, helpless.

"Dog down. Backup NOW!" Vader shouted. Swinging into action, he moved wide out into the yard, circling the man, buying time. Nose drawn up in a snarl, teeth exposed, saliva dripping, Vader was terrible to see. A deep bark and the man turned to see a bear coming up under the fence. He rubbed his eyes. Did inhaling bear spray make you see bears? It was not much of a relief to realize that it was actually a dog. An angry Rottweiler now hovered on his flank, just out of spray range. More dogs poured up out of the holes and back into the yard. The man understood the odds. He backed toward his porch, then turned and ran.

Still unable to open his burning eyes, Charlie felt powerful jaws grab the loose fur at the back of his neck. He knew Flint's grip. Like a fallen teddy bear, Charlie was lifted and dragged through the tunnel and out into the alley. Taking deep gulps of the cleaner air, still gasping, his breath came easier.

Abandoning his lookout post, Max slid through

the dogs to Charlie's side. First licking then spitting, he attacked the contaminated fur around Charlie's eyes. Charlie lay limp, wheezing.

"Torpedo here. I'm sooooo sorry. It's my fault. My fault," he said, putting his mouth directly to Charlie's ear.

"Not so loud, friend. My ears are fine," said Charlie.

Torpedo backed away, anxious.

"Good news about bugs though, right? Right Torpedo? Right?" said Hank looking at the worried Dalmatian.

Flint spoke up, "Hank's right. When Vader called us, you crawled back and forth over that bug a couple of times. You rubbed your belly all over that beetle. You worried about Charlie and forgot to be scared. Pretty brave."

Torpedo wagged his tail slowly.

Rocky gazed first at Nautilus then at Torpedo and spoke for the first time.

"Huh. Brown's not a usual Dalmatian color. More common to see the white with dark spots," he said, staring at the two of them. Identical expressions of horror crossed the Dalmatian faces.

Charlie's eyes opened, blurred. He turned toward Nautilus and Torpedo. Two brown dogs came into focus. They bristled with wet mud and smelled like a damp cellar. A stunned beetle, likely the one of interest, clung to Torpedo's chest fur. As Charlie watched, the beetle dropped to the ground and strolled away.

Charlie made an odd sound in his throat. The worried animals turned in his direction. His breathing seemed comfortable. Sugar, following Charlie's gaze, also witnessed the beetle's escape. She giggled. Charlie's throat sounds evolved into a hiccup and then a chuckle.

"Don't laugh, Sugar. You're the same chocolate color as Drucker right now," said Lava staring at Sugar. Her show dog smile widened into a huge grin.

It was contagious. Max, Flint, Drucker, Hank, Rocky, and finally the twins, joined. They giggled madly as they took in their muddy coats. Giggling turned to laughter as they revisited the man's hasty retreat in his dirty socks. They ribbed Rocky for the ridiculous timing of his howl and their sides ached over the beetle that loved and lost Torpedo. Mostly they laughed with relief. Everyone was safe.

Only Vader did not let down his guard. Turning to Charlie he said, "You came back for me."

"Always," said Charlie simply.

Vader nodded. Rocky watched his rescuers, his thin tail thumping.

"Rocky, we're glad to have you with us. For now, you'll be Lava's wingman. She'll explain," said Charlie.

The animals, tired now, fell into a single file and headed for the docks and sleep. Charlie trotted at the head of the column. Vader moved into the formation this time, second in command, directly behind Charlie. Max took his own way home.

In the weeks after Rocky's rescue Lava pushed for something new.

"Together, all of us, we are something. We can be a band or a team. We can organize so that we are ready," said Lava.

"Ready for what?" asked Hank bouncing around the outside of the group.

"Anything, everything. I don't know," said Lava.

"This soldier agrees. Rocky is free because of all of us. And Max is alive," said Vader.

"It's true. Charlie couldn't have done it alone. He needed everyone's voices to save me," said Max. He shivered, remembering the icy hold.

"But what else? Huh? What is our squad going to do?" asked Hank.

Drucker leaned forward. "We stopped people from littering our beach because we *noticed.* I think we should form a group that watches. After that, we can see what the tide brings," he said.

Charlie nodded toward the chocolate lab. "Yes. The first step is always to watch."

And so it was decided. A band was formed. Max suggested they call it "First Watch." The group asked Charlie to serve as general and he agreed. Life on the dock returned to an easy, predictable rhythm. Fishing boats came and went loaded with their catch. The ocean breeze filled the warm air with salt and seaweed. The days flowed. Everything was the same, and everything was different. The watch had begun.

RED ANIMAL

Trouble arrived at the dock on a black evening, way past midnight. A shrouded half-moon struggled to be seen and eyes could only pick out shadows. Misty rain blew through the rigging of Charlie's boat and he sensed the dry grass smell of Max approaching.

Abruptly, the gate at the far end of the dock grated open. Three men began moving quietly down the wooden walk. Max jumped onto the boat deck; his gleaming eyes the only thing Charlie could see in the darkness. They crouched low as the men passed. Sweat, unwashed clothing, and cigar smoke sharpened the air. The trio boarded a dilapidated tugboat, not far down the dock. A single dim light hung in a cabin so small that the men were forced to stay huddled outside on

Three men began moving quietly down the wooden walk.

the deck. One of the men lifted a tarp to reveal a haphazard pile of nets, gloves, and bins. They each grabbed some of the equipment. As the rain picked up, Charlie strained to hear the low voices.

"Those turtle eggs will be ready soon. I've never seen so many turtles laying eggs on the same beach. We'll have buckets of hatchlings to sell . . . we won't even know what to do with all that lovely money!" The speaker turned slightly and the light bounced off a jagged scar on his cheek. A gray nylon cap stretched tightly over his forehead. "And Nitro," said the same voice sounding annoyed now, "remember you gotta be more careful this time. It's easy to smash the turtles and then we can't sell them. Those huge boots of yours are lethal weapons. So watch it!"

"I'd rather have these big old feet than a face that got dragged through a cheese grater!" said a deep voice in response. "Besides, if I step on the little critters, who really cares? Hundreds will be hatching this time. Why worry if I crush one or two?" continued his companion as he pushed a cascade of soggy black hair away from his eyes.

There was an uneasy silence for a minute and then, "Lots of money when we sell them. Like picking money right up off the beach," squeaked the third man, his entire face buried under a baggy red hood.

"Dangerous . . . could be prison . . . keep it quiet . . . coast guard patrols protect turtles," snatches of speech drifted in the air. As the three men spoke, the story became clearer.

Weeks ago, Tex, their scout, had witnessed green turtle mothers as they climbed out of the sea. A full moon had allowed glimpses of their wet backs and spotlighted them as they buried their leathery white eggs.

The hatchlings would be ready when the moon was full. Each turtle would break from its shell; dig up to the surface of the beach and then dash for the safety of the sea. But the poachers would be waiting. The hatchlings would be caught up, helpless, in large nets and buckets. Instead of the cool ocean they would go to animal collectors, soup pots in exotic restaurants, or in amulets and potions for dark arts.

Silent horror overtook Charlie, but Max spoke first.

"It's them, the poachers we've been hearing about," hissed Max, "We must stop this! The green turtles are endangered. There aren't enough left in the wild," he said in a rising tone.

"Shh, they'll hear you, Max," Charlie said. Suddenly it was quiet on the deck of the old tug.

"Hey, what was that sound?" asked an anxious high-pitched voice.

"Would you settle down, Squeaky? It was just a dog," was the deep rumbling response from Nitro. Talk among the men resumed.

"What did I tell you about trusting your partners?" asked Tex pulling his gray beanie off and wringing it out. "Listen up, Squeaky! I'll go over everything, real slow. This is how it works: as they hatch, turtles move toward the brightest light they can find. Usually, that's the full moon on the waves, but we'll trick them. The shine of our truck

A full moon spotlighted them as they buried their leathery white eggs.

headlights will be stronger and they'll turn away from the ocean and right into our nets!"

The two friends eavesdropped on the details of the plan for some time. Finally, the men filed down the dock to leave, brushing close to the sailboat. Squeaky, peering under his dripping hood, looked directly toward Charlie as he passed. He jumped back with a yelp, bumping his fellow poachers who both staggered.

"What's wrong with you?" asked an irritated Tex, "You darn near pushed me in the water!"

"I'm not sure. But I saw something. It looked red. Maybe an animal or . . . " Squeaky peered nervously into the gloom.

"Idiot! A red animal, on a dock? In the middle of the night? More likely you saw the inside of your own hood. Come on, let's get out of this storm," said Nitro.

And with that, clutching their gear, they put their heads down in the wind and left. The gate banged shut behind them. Raindrops quivered on Charlie's short copper eyelashes. Max licked the drops away and waited. Charlie stood up, "Gather 'First Watch.' Emergency meeting in the morning," he said, "Make sure everyone is there." Then he headed belowdecks and out of the rain.

FIRST WATCH

A clear dawn chased away the storm. The mist of whales' breath and roasting coffee danced in the breeze. First Watch took every meeting seriously. Dog after dog, they responded to Charlie's call. Flint's muscles rippled as he sauntered up. He was accompanied by Hank who spit out so many questions that he hardly breathed. Dark Drucker and golden Sugar, already gleaming with ocean water from a morning swim, breezed in next. Lava and her red hound wingman, arrived punctually. Rocky, head down, sniffed his way toward the group, lost in all the scents of the morning. Finally, Vader sidled up, giving a curt military nod to the others. The Dalmatian twins, somewhat predictably, overslept.

Charlie called the meeting to order. Even from a distance, one clearly saw that he commanded the

respect of all. He lay on the sailboat deck, slightly above the others. As his instinct dictated, front paws precisely crossed, he faced the dock gate and any possible approaching danger.

"Looks like we've got poachers," he announced. The dogs were silent. "Sounds like they plan to net green turtle hatchlings and sell them." There was a rising murmur of anger among the assembled dogs.

"Cowards!" said Flint, "What kind of poachers are these? Baby turtles are totally defenseless."

"Torpedo here! Yeah! Turtles hatch at night so that seabirds and crabs don't eat them."

"They're so small they can fall into a man's footprint," said Lava.

"Trapped in a footprint?" asked Rocky with disbelief.

Hank raised his voice, "Green turtles are endangered. Hey, right Vader? If their population gets too small . . . that's it for them. No way back. Gone forever."

"You're right Hank. They could go extinct," said Vader.

Charlie continued as if he had not been interrupted, "These poachers are cunning. They watch the turtle mothers as they come up to lay their eggs. They realize that studying turtle habits gives them an advantage."

"How much time do we have Charlie?" asked Drucker, who always preferred to plan ahead.

"The next full moon is in less than one week, not much time at all," said Charlie.

At that, a storm of voices rose from the group.

"But that's not enough time to find out where the eggs are!"

"What are we going to do?"

It was hard to know who said what amidst all the loud voices. Charlie waited calmly, white paws still crossed, unruffled.

"I've been working on a plan," he said decisively. "It'll take three squads. Flint, I'll depend on you and Vader to get the power dogs together. Sugar, you and Drucker have just five days to prepare a band of surfers for action," he said, "And boards. We'll need extra surfboards to pull it off."

The animals waited, uncertain.

"I'll take charge of the trackers. Rocky, you're with me," continued Charlie nodding at the Redbone Hound. "And Max, you, as always are the eyes and ears of the operation. The first thing I want you to consider is a solution to those truck headlights," he said, glancing toward the cat who sat unblinking by his side.

Glancing from face to attentive face, Charlie finally leaned forward and shared the details of his plan.

After the meeting, Flint left first, a powerful snarl on his massive face. Hank danced and wove at his heels, a blur of gray-and-white fur. A constant stream of words drifted backward along the dock.

"Dangerous. Crazy. Scary but . . . right, Flint?" asked Hank, hardly taking a breath. "But you and Vader can show them who is in charge, right Vader?" He glanced back as Vader slid into a patrol position at the rear. Vader briefly exposed all the sharp teeth on the left side of his ebony face. Deciding to respect Vader's need for quiet, Hank fell silent as they all trotted out through the gate.

Next to leave were Sugar and Drucker, debating whether *just any* dog can learn to surf. Close on their heels bounced a very excited Bulldog and two uncertain Dalmatian brothers. The newly formed waterdog squad promised to meet at the beach once the Labs had collected extra boards.

Charlie and Rocky stayed behind on the sailboat. Thanks to Max, they suspected that the poachers worked in a warehouse at the edge of town. The whole plan hinged on the two trackers. They needed to locate the exact beach where the mother turtles had secretly buried their eggs.

NINJAS

L ess than a day later, the afternoon cooled into a scented evening. A waxing moon rose as Charlie and Rocky took up positions outside a crumbling warehouse.

"Like dark shadows tonight Rocky. We're Ninjas," instructed Charlie. A breeze stirred the pale fur in his ears.

Rocky whimpered with barely controlled excitement as they waited in the dim light. The smells of frying fish and roasting meat, from a nearby market, touched their noses.

"Remember, no noise," said Charlie. "Alerting the poachers to our presence could destroy our plans."

Suddenly his head came up. Three men had stepped out through the rusted door of the building

"Like dark shadows tonight, Rocky. We're ninjas," instructed Charlie.

and were clearly visible. Their now familiar scents assailed him. Sour sweat, dirty clothes, and old cigars slapped his nostrils. Although glimpsed only briefly, on a dark night, his nose confirmed that these were definitely the same men. He nodded firmly at Rocky. Rocky caught the distinct smells too and struggled not to sing aloud as Redbone Hounds do when they pick up an important trail.

"We're ghost trackers, silence itself," Charlie said in an urgent whisper, "Follow my lead."

With visible effort, Rocky controlled his voice and was still.

At a distance, the dogs watched the poachers buy hot fish and plantains for their dinner. The men ambled down a palm-fringed road, noisily smacking their lips and licking their fingers, heading toward the ocean.

"Wait . . . did you see that? "Squeaky suddenly yelled, "I saw it again. It's a small red animal. It looks like . . . a fox. I think it's following us!"

The two dogs crouched back into the shadows and exchanged worried glances. Nitro and Tex laughed at Squeaky.

"I think your brain is cooking inside that hood you wear, Squeaky. Your crazy imagination is getting on my nerves. Actually *you*, Squeaky, are getting on my nerves! Tell me, how many other animals have you seen spying on us today?" asked Nitro shaking his curly head. Nitro and Tex laughed until one of them choked on a piece of plantain. The teasing of Squeaky continued, as they walked along.

Charlie and Rocky lagged behind in the dusk until the men finally arrived at a quiet beach. Trees crouched snugly around a cove. This was it! The very beach that Charlie had been hoping to find. Now, the dogs knew where the mother turtles had patiently deposited their eggs. The warm sand stretched to the ocean with no hint of the tiny creatures that were buried beneath.

The poachers seated themselves on the beach and continued eating.

"Less than a week now," said Tex, loudly slurping up his dinner.

"Agreed. We've got a three-quarter moon tonight, and it will be a full moon soon," came Nitro's deep voice. He spilled food on his dirty shirt, and the fumes from his clothes annoyed Charlie's nose.

"We're going to get enough turtles this time that we could even retire for a while. Go into hiding, live it up, and enjoy spending all our money," Tex said. "I could take it real easy and maybe start a school for poachers or something. Our motto could be, 'Mess with Mother Nature and Make Money.' What do you think Nitro? I mean, if I can make a poacher out of Squeaky, I could probably teach any idiot," Tex rambled on.

Suddenly Squeaky yelped frantically, "YIKES . . . something just brushed my leg,"

Rocky slithered low and away from the men, back toward Charlie in the tree line.

"My fish! Where is my other piece of fish?" howled Squeaky.

"Maybe a 'land' shark took it," said Tex moving his feet and sending a distinct sweaty sock odor adrift on the breeze.

Squeaky leaped to his feet, pulled his hood off, and glared down at his companions. The men began quarreling loudly. Rocky avoided Charlie's eyes but felt quite proud of the delicacy with which he had slid that fish right off the edge of the wrapper. Voices raised angrily, the poachers finally left the beach. Rocky's skinny tail wagged gently as he meandered behind Charlie, back to the dock and home.

BRAINPOWER

"**D**isaster!" shouted Drucker as he and Sugar watched their students out in the surf. "This plan of Charlie's is not going to work. We can't get these rookies ready in time. We just plain can't!" he said hopelessly.

Sugar secretly agreed, but she kept quiet. The morning had started well enough. Lava, her forehead wrinkled with concentration, along with Torpedo and Nautilus, had joined them at the beach. They had started the instruction on land.

"The goal out there is NOT to swim. The goal is to ride! Stay in the middle of your surfboard. If you stand too far forward, your board will become a submarine. If you're too far back, the nose will come up and you'll do a wheelie. We don't want swimmers out there. We need riders!" drilled Sugar, walking along the lineup of surfboards on the sand.

Next, the knot of dogs moved to the shallow water lapping at the shoreline. Drucker and Sugar demonstrated on their boards, balancing expertly in waves they called ankle-breakers.

To everyone's surprise, this phase went smoothly. Both the Dalmatian twins and Lava were naturals. They quickly mastered the technique and balance. Hours later they were ready to head out to the real surf.

"Listen up!" said Drucker, "Canine surfing, with human assist, is common."

"Nautilus here. I've seen how it works. People hold a board in the shallows; the dog hops on and gets a push into the surf. Catches a big wave and rides back to the beach. Easy."

Drucker continued, "Surfing 'human free' is another matter entirely, and that's what you need to learn today. Most dogs will never master it. Just aren't equipped with the brainpower or the timing."

"Torpedo here. Nautilus and I have plenty of

brains. You and Sugar surf without human help and we can too. Tell us the secret."

"If you want to surf without people, then you have to pick a launch site that takes human hands out of the equation. It needs to work for paws. That's the secret," said Drucker.

Sugar stared into the distance, "Exactly. Do you all see that finger of land that sticks way out into the ocean? Launch a board from there and you are already in big waves. That point of land divides the rollers like a knife. Some waves are forced past to the north and some to the south. Take off from that spit, choose your angle, and you can land on any of the beaches."

"Okay, let's go get some waves. Grab that strap on the back of your board with your teeth. We are going to pull the boards behind us," said Drucker.

"Human surfers call this strap a 'leash'. No, I'm not kidding," Sugar said, in response to the disbelieving looks. "Now, let's get moving."

Not wanting to be a dog without brainpower, each of them set to the task of locating the leash and getting into the pull position.

"Nautilus here. This is stupid people stuff. I can't even find my leash."

"Torpedo here. Check under your board, that's where I found mine," said his brother.

The Dalmatians were a jumble of twisted rope and panting frustration.

"Nautilus, the leash goes along the side of your body, not between your legs," growled Drucker. And then under his breath, "Disaster!"

The two Labradors waited, straps between their teeth. Their lines curved elegantly along their flanks to the boards behind them, ready to pull.

"How did you set up so fast?" complained Lava who had grabbed her leash, and a big bite of sand along with it. Sand clung to her nose and wet lips. "It's not natural."

"You'll get it," said Sugar. "Don't forget, we're service dogs. As teenagers, we learned to open doors, answer phones and help people with their clothes. Our man depends on Drucker and me." said Sugar.

"Yup," said Drucker trying hard not to look at

the twins. "So, dragging a surfboard into launch position is not our biggest challenge."

Finally, straps grasped properly, and boards slithering behind them, the dogs walked out onto the sharp point of land. The thin sliver of the bank split the ocean water, sending waves north and south, just as Sugar had described. A dog had only to pick a direction. Sugar demonstrated first. At the launch site, she dropped her leash and gauged the waves that would send her to the northern beaches. Seeing her wave approach, she head-butted the board over the embankment. Demonstrating perfect timing, she slid low and fast onto the rocking board. An offshore breeze made for perfect, clean waves. With the skill of many years, Sugar caught her chosen wave and rode, close to the curl. Drucker followed suit and impressed the watching students as he "shot the barrel" and was lost from sight, riding inside the hollow tube of a wave.

Torpedo and Nautilus plunged in, whining with excitement, eager to give it a try. In seconds, both of them lost their boards in high-flying wheelies and were tossed into the surf. Lava stayed up half a second longer, and then she too was thrown barking into the water.

Charlie breezed up, joined the two Labs, and watched the chaos. Uncontrolled surfboards popped up out of the waves and one nearly hit Nautilus in the head. A riderless board slid right over the top of swimming Lava, while Torpedo gulped seawater and paddled furiously.

"Complete amateurs!" moaned Drucker, "Someone is going to get killed out there. We're pushing these dogs too fast."

"They're going to get it, my friend," said Charlie, "They have excellent teachers. Both you and Sugar have surfed for years. They just need time."

Sugar nodded hesitantly, and they watched together as the students launched their boards back into the swells for a second time. There was no improvement. The Dalmatian twins crashed into each other in a blur of spots and were immediately swimming in foam. Lava never managed to get up on her board at all, and a wave sent her spinning underwater. Drucker's tail drooped with disappointment, but Charlie looked undaunted.

"They've got heart, Drucker," said Charlie, "Look at the courage out there. It's going to work! You'll see." And then, to everyone's surprise, he joined the lessons in the surf.

As the day lengthened, those on the beach were unaware that they were being quietly observed. Vader watched the events from a camouflaged position. With years of tactical experience, he had carefully considered the military risks of Charlie's plan.

As he watched the tumbling, barking dogs, he shook his head. The danger was significant. The plan demanded that they outwit ruthless men, in poor visibility, with inadequate training. The operation would occur in heavy ocean swells, and timing had to be precise. He bared his long teeth, then crouched down in the green shade and melted into the trees.

THE CHALLENGE

The next few days passed swiftly as the teams made their preparations. The biggest flurry continued to be out on the surfing beach. The dogs practiced their skills. Each time they were tossed off their surfboards and denied a full ride, they tried again.

All the efforts began to pay off. Lava could now stick to her board like glue, riding fully upright with sturdy legs slightly bent. Charlie was pleased when the Dalmatian twins tied for the longest ride, without a fall. Sugar demonstrated admirable tube-riding. Drucker, so well known on the surfing circuit, was truly enviable with his unique stance. Balancing, head lower than tail, he was a master in turbulent water. Each dog worked hard and, in the final days, mastered some rough swells. All

Each time they were tossed off their surfboards and denied a full ride, they tried again.

appeared to be going according to plan. They were as close to ready as time would allow.

That very evening, Charlie had two visitors aboard his boat, one of them quite unexpected. His neighbor, Max, came by for sunset. They sat quietly together on the foredeck. As darkness fell, the second visitor arrived. Vader appeared suddenly and without warning. He eased smoothly up onto the deck. The three animals nodded to each other in greeting and Charlie waited for Vader to speak.

"Your plan puts 'First Watch' in jeopardy. The risk is unacceptable," Vader said without preamble. "There is potential to lose lives. Abort this mission." Vader's ears flattened as he spoke.

Charlie gazed steadily at Vader without moving a muscle. Then he shifted his attention to Max.

"And you, my friend? What do you think?" Charlie asked.

"Vader and I, all of us, we follow your lead. You've united us into a group that's powerful together. But deep down, I worry that your past haunts you. It drives you to recklessness," Max trailed off. "We deserve to hear your story, Charlie."

Vader growled and leaned fiercely toward Charlie. "I don't want to talk of nightmares or the past! Time is short. The assault plan exposes our dogs on all flanks. There are limits to what animals can do here. Let the coast guard handle this one."

The metal gate at the end of the dock suddenly clanged shut, interrupting their talk. A familiar figure, with a heavy limp, moved slowly along the dock toward them. Silence fell as they watched him walk wearily along the creaking planks. Captain Kegun Hatsukami seemed to be having more pain in his leg tonight, and he stopped to rest before he climbed aboard the sailboat. Once up on the deck, he glanced absent-mindedly at Vader and Max and then squatted beside Charlie. He stroked Charlie's thick coat for a few moments and then headed belowdecks. Pans clanged, and the smell of frying onions, garlic, and ginger wafted up out of the cabin.

"Are the coast guard any closer to the turtle poachers?" asked Max.

"No," said Charlie, "They don't have the reconnaissance we do. They still don't know who the men are, and they definitely don't know the location of the beach where the poachers plan to strike next."

Vader shifted his body with frustration, "But Cap lives with you, Charlie! Doesn't he have any idea what you're doing?"

"Cap and I have been together for a long time. My story is also his story. He would do anything for me. But humans do not see us as we dogs see each other. He does not see what we, all of us, can do together," Charlie said.

The silence lengthened. No further explanation was needed. The animals understood that while Cap loved Charlie, he had no awareness that he shared a sailboat with a warrior dog, a descendant from a long line of warriors.

The moon rose slowly and bathed the three friends with its light. They sniffed the delicious aromas of Cap's dinner. Finally, Vader rose to his feet.

As Vader turned to go, Charlie spoke up, "You're both right. The danger is greater than we have faced before. And Max, perhaps the time *has* come for me to share my story. After that, each animal may consider their own decision."

"I will call the squads for a meeting at daybreak," said Vader crisply, and then he slid off along the moonlit dock.

Max stayed longer, sitting close to Charlie. Lights in the nearby boats slowly extinguished for the evening. The darkness closed in.

CHARLIE'S STORY

Along, restless night later, Charlie climbed down from his sailboat and joined the hushed, waiting dogs. Everyone was there. He moved into their midst and the circle closed around him. The dogs leaned in until only the tips of Charlie's triangular ears rose above their heads. He spoke slowly as if he could not see them, his eyes focused on the past. He spoke in pictures that burned in their minds and lingered long after the exact words were forgotten.

Summer nights come slowly to the sea islands of the North. The light lingers and twilight goes on forever. It's green and cool up there. Back then, Cap patrolled the remote coasts and coves as a park ranger. At the close of each day, he climbed into a small open motorboat to do his rounds. He carried a radio and a flare gun, and he always took Charlie along.

On this particular evening, the patrol was routine. Cap pulled up some illegal crab pots and, at one point, gave directions to some hikers along the shore. The boat approached the last cove in the route, flying across the water. The air rushed at Charlie's nose, filled with the scent of pine, ferns, and moss. He sat, as he always did, in the bow of the boat, head straight into the wind. Cap hit full throttle and they picked up speed. The wind forced Charlie's eyelids shut and pushed his ears flat.

As their boat curved into that last cove, the sharp smell of blood hit Charlie's nostrils, overpowering all other scents. It was hot and unmistakable. Turning to Cap, he barked, short and high, giving a warning. Cap slowed their speed but moved without hesitation toward a boat anchored in the deep water of the inlet. Several tall dark fins stood, like trees, on the water. The fins were moving constantly around the boat. The boat itself listed to starboard from a weight that was strapped along the side.

Men strained and hoisted, adjusting a large stretcher to support what they had captured. As Cap and Charlie came closer, they could see an ensnared baby Orca whale. Although still young, its size made the fishing trawler tilt as they tried to get it aboard. Where the straps leashed its black-and-white flanks, small drops of blood misted the air and fell into the water.

The baby's mouth opened and Charlie saw a pink-and-black spotted mouth with rows of perfect white teeth. Its dark eyes watched the pod of whales that circled in the waves below. A high-pitched distress call sounded from the pod and one of the tall fins rushed toward the boat.

An alarmed call went out from the men, "Brace yourselves! The mother is circling back again. Watch out!"

At the last moment, the mother swerved and created a massive wave of water, tipping the boat violently. The men shouted and clung tightly to avoid being pitched overboard. That's when two of the straps broke under the strain. The baby jerked abruptly downward, closer to the water.

Cap should have radioed for backup. He had no weapons. But things were moving too quickly. He did the only thing he could do. He stood up, took aim, and fired his flare gun directly at the poachers' boat. White-hot burning light showered over the wallowing boat. More frantic yelling as the men turned to see Cap and Charlie bearing down on them. With all the rocking, another rope slid off the baby. It dangled on the stretcher, tail in the air, like a giant toddler about to go down a slide. There was only one strap left in place.

"It's the coast guard!" someone yelled.

"No, it's a park ranger. So he doesn't have a gun!" said another.

"Well then shoot, idiot! Shoot! Shoot him!" said a voice rising out of the din.

Gunfire filled the twilight. The men turned their weapons and all of their attention on Cap and Charlie. Their boat slid to a gradual standstill as they threw themselves down flat. Charlie lay still,

It dangled on the stretcher, tail in the air,
like a giant toddler about to go down a slide.

bullets whizzing overhead. Orca calls rose from the pod followed by loud human curses. Seeing the opportunity, the mother Orca whale had separated from the pod and rushed the boat again.

Booming voices and chaos, "Stabilize the load or it'll overturn the boat! I don't want to go into the water with those monsters."

Another shouted command, "Stabilize that whale or cut it loose. You idiots have already injured it. Those wounds will leave scars and buyers don't like that."

And then frantically, "Cut it loose! Cut it loose! We're going over!"

The last rope was cut. The baby made a thunderous splash as it slid face-first back into the water. The trawler's engine roared and the poachers fled the cove.

Charlie sensed something warm on the floor of his boat and realized that it was blood, Cap's blood. Cap lay very still. He had been hit. Likely, he was an easy target when he stood to fire the flare gun. His leg was very bad. Crawling toward the radio, Charlie pressed the emergency channel and then pulled himself carefully up onto Cap's leg. He pressed his weight down firmly, to slow the bleeding. The towering bodies of the pod rocked the small open boat as they passed. Surrounded by their protective family, the baby Orca and his mother submerged. Powerless, Charlie lay there on Cap's bleeding leg. He crouched in the bottom of that bobbing boat, filled with fear. If the poachers circled back, he had no defense, no weapon. He did not even have a plan. Both of their lives depended on Charlie but he cringed, terrified, hoping for someone . . . anyone else, to take charge.

When the coast guard finally arrived, they found Charlie and Cap drifting in the silent cove. Whale blood still floated on the water. Cap's blood colored Charlie's fur and puddled on the floor of the boat. Charlie, and the rescuers, did not think that Cap would live.

When Charlie got to this point in the story he paused and took a ragged breath. His eyes were half-closed and his voice shook. The listening dogs remained mute, stunned into silence. Drucker wiped his eyes. Edging between the dogs, Max drew as close as he could to Charlie.

It was Hank who spoke first, "But the baby whale didn't die, right Charlie? And Cap is still here. Safe and sound, living on the sailboat with you Charlie. Right, Charlie? Right?"

Charlie responded slowly as if suddenly aware of the dogs around him. "You're right Hank. The whales escaped and, as you all know, Cap did not die. But it was close. It took months for him to walk again and he will always have a limp. After that, Cap changed. He was angry. All he wanted was a chance to fight poachers, like those men. Joining the coast guard was how he was going to do it. As for me, cowering in the bottom of that boat, covered with Cap's blood changed me too. I never again wanted to be waiting, weak and unprepared, for someone else to take the initiative against evil. I made a pledge. That very night, I vowed to lead an offensive life, to take a stand."

"Your bowing and chanting . . . " Flint

murmured. Nautilus and Torpedo nodded in unison.

Max repeated aloud the words they all knew so well, "I am a sentry at our planet's gate. I watch and wait. With a soldier's heart and strength, I pledge to protect the unprotected."

Silence reigned again among the circle of attentive animals as the harbor waves slapped the dock.

Finally, Vader spoke, "I will stand with you, no matter the risks, covering your flank in battle."

Abruptly everyone spoke at once, filling the air around Charlie.

Flint, and then each of the others, promised support for the battle ahead. The last to respond was Lava, barely visible among the legs of the taller animals.

"I'm not big but I feel taller being a part of all of you. Those poachers are gonna be real sorry they ever met this dog!" she said with a snarl.

Chuckles followed. The serious mood lifted and the group began to break up. As they left, each dog paused in front of Charlie with a nod of respect. Charlie rested quietly, exhausted from reliving his story. Long after the others had gone, Max remained. The two friends lay so close that Charlie could feel the beating of Max's heart.

THE EDGE OF BATTLE

At long last, the moon bloomed into round fullness. The time had arrived. All three squads gathered for a final meeting. Excited, and anxious talk filled the air.

Charlie spoke, "Listen up everyone. Thanks to Flint's family garden shed, we've borrowed some lanterns. Battery-powered and push button. Waterdogs, notice that the handle is a large metal ring. Scoop the handle up with your lower jaw and let it hang there."

"It'll be secure behind your front teeth, like hanging a coat on a hook," said Flint. "Be sure to push it on before you pick it up."

"Flint, Vader and Hank, are you clear on the plan? Are your voices and teeth ready?" Charlie asked. "Rocky, remember, we're depending on your howl to give the signal. Waterdogs Sugar, Drucker, Lava, Torpedo, and Nautilus, lights on!" directed Charlie. Then, lifting a lantern out of the pile, he said firmly, "Tonight I will be joining you in the ocean."

A murmur of surprise rose from the gathered dogs. Charlie was a tracker. They all recognized that it was his nose that led them first to the poachers and then to the location of the precious eggs. And although he had joined the training in the surf, he was not naturally a water dog.

"We need all the dogs on the water that we can get," said Charlie, and it was settled.

Charlie turned to Max, "Keep your distance my friend. Stay safe."

"I will be in the shadows, right there with you," responded Max looking at each of the anxious faces around him.

Not far away, on the beach, the full moon had sent nature's signal to the hatchlings far beneath the sand. Deep in their snug dark nests, the baby turtles began breaking out of their shells. By the dozens, they dug up to the bright beach. Once on the sand, their heads turned toward the moon glinting on the surf. And just as nature had planned, they ran, tiny race cars headed for the sea.

"Okay boys! Turn on the headlights," yelled Nitro.

He and his cronies had been lying in wait, for hours, in the darkness. The bright headlights of the Dodge truck illuminated the beach and the hundreds of moving green hatchlings. As one, the turtles paused. They spun in confusion. Their genetic instructions told them to seek the light and move quickly toward it. This ancient code helped them to get safely into the sea. The true beacon should be the full moon, on the tumbling surf, guiding them away from predators on land. But now, they began to swarm in the direction of the headlights, away from the ocean and toward danger.

"It's working! They're turning!" bellowed Nitro.

"Of course it's working! Get the nets and start scooping them up. Watch those big feet of yours.

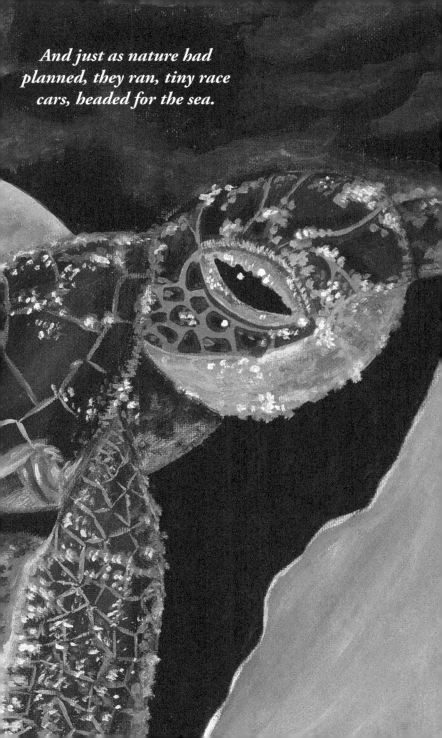

And just as nature had planned, they ran, tiny race cars, headed for the sea.

You almost smashed one," said Tex.

The poachers brought out nylon nets and caught dozens of turtles with each swipe along the sand. As he wielded a sandy net, Nitro began whooping and laughing loudly.

"It's just plain ridiculous how easy this is!" he hollered across the beach. "It's piles of money, and all of it is running as fast as it can, right toward me!" and he burst into more laughter.

"Keep working you idiot! Try to remember, this is the biggest hatch we may ever see. We gotta make the most of it," said Tex, turning so that for a moment the scar on his face was a snake in the moonlight.

"Tiny dollar bills, are you asking me to pick you up? Yes, I think you are," crooned Squeaky to his victims. "Little pieces of money with shiny eyes and wiggly legs, would you like to get into my net?" went his singsong. "Come on. Up you go. Look at all those green faces staring at me. Hey! They got faces but no brains, right Tex?" asked Squeaky, delighted with this thought.

"*Get the nets and start scooping them up.*"

Ignored by his partners, he began babbling to himself again, "Cuz you are too dumb to know that some of you might go into a soup pot and get EATEN," he roared into the net full of frightened hatchlings.

After that, the beach fell quiet as the poachers worked steadily. Nets brimming with babies, they dumped them into large bins and went back to catch more.

That is when something out on the ocean began to glow. Faint at first, it steadied and became stronger. Circles of light appeared just beyond the surf and hovered in the air. First, there was a single light, then another, and another, and yet still another emerged from the darkness. The lights were moving toward the beach, floating fast. More dazzling than the moonlight, they rushed toward the shore. The hatchlings on the sand hesitated for a second time, uncertain, torn between the truck lights and the new beckoning shine in the surf.

"Why are the turtles stopping? What is that light in the waves?" Tex asked uncertainly, eyes

Circles of light appeared
just beyond the surf
and hovered in the air

fixed on the oncoming glow.

"It's the coast guard, they found us!" screeched Squeaky, and he dropped his net and began backing toward the truck.

"RELAX! Whatever this is, it's not the coast guard. But it's ruining our plan. Let's get the bins in the truck. We've got plenty of money here already," said Nitro.

Then the commotion began. It started with a long drawn-out song. The voice of a Redbone Hound filled the night. The next instant Vader and Flint leaped snarling out of the trees, right along with Rocky. They launched at the men holding the bins of turtles.

Terrified, the poachers stumbled back. The bins fell, spilling the turtles back onto the sand. Hank pushed onto the scene, nipping fiercely at pants, shirts, and socks. The poachers shrank away from the herding dog. Shaking and clinging to each other they knotted tightly together.

Hank panted excitedly, "I got it! It's an all-clear. I got it locked up," as he circled the poachers.

Then the commotion began.

"Nice work, partner," said Flint, over his shoulder, as he moved toward the old Dodge truck. Vader followed, ominous. Sitting up tall, they placed themselves directly in front of the glaring headlights. They created a perfect body block and extinguished the light.

LANTERNS

Ocean waves brought the moving lights swiftly closer, and now shapes and figures came into view. Dogs, many dogs it seemed, were rushing forward with flickering lanterns hanging from their jaws. They rode their surfboards with expert skill. Bright board colors and silver water flashed.

"It's . . . it's . . . aliens! The aliens have landed," croaked Squeaky.

"No, you dummy. It's NOT aliens, it's dogs. Some kind of crazy surfing dogs," said Nitro.

With perfect balance, Drucker, Sugar, Lava, and the Dalmatian twins slid along the waves. Showing off, Lava "dropped in" and stole a wave from Torpedo who nearly dropped his light to bark. Charlie came last, riding his board with ease, tail

"Some kind of crazy surfing dogs."

tightly curled, his eyes on the target. The lanterns lit up the roiling sprint of hatchlings and the faceoff between dogs and poachers on the beach.

Sliding from waves to sand, the water dogs stepped off their boards. Lanterns held tightly in their teeth they raised their heads high, creating a wall of light. The effect was immediate. Confused no longer, the delighted baby turtles swung like a flock of birds back to the ocean. They plunged into the water, splashing around the surfboards and between the dogs' paws. Soon, they covered the water's edge and the surging waves like green skipping stones. And still they kept coming. The water washed the sand from their pointed noses and off their patterned shells. They blinked their black eyes at the dogs as they headed deeper into their watery home.

"Who cares about the money!" shouted Nitro, "We need to get out of here!"

He picked up a large piece of wood. The others, understanding the plan, grabbed sharp sticks and rocks. Backs to each other they faced Hank and Rocky.

"We have to make it to the truck. Those big dogs are busy, blocking the headlights, so we've got a chance," said Tex.

Squeaky flicked open a wicked looking switchblade and stared at Hank. "I've got an ugly surprise for them," he said, pale and scared.

The first stone pelted Rocky squarely in the chest. The poachers cheered when he let out a yelp.

"That's right you beasts! No coast guard here yet. These dogs can't hold us 'till the morning and they know it," said Nitro, swinging his club at Hank.

At that moment, a piercing sound exploded over the beach. It swept upward, a shattering, deafening high-pitched wail. A sound that split the eardrum.

"I see it! I can see it! There it is again," moaned a horrified Squeaky.

Tex and Nitro turned, searching the chaotic battlefield, seeing nothing at first.

"It's the red fox. It's him. There he is. Over there. Can you see him now?" Squeaky said, his pointer finger shaking. "He's been trying to stop us! From the beginning!"

Charlie stood regally in the moonlight, lantern lying at his feet. Ocean water and powdered sand clung to his face and incoming waves curled around his white toes. He held his body stiff and his powerful shoulders solid. The wild sound exploded from his mouth. It was not a cry that any creature on that beach had ever heard. It did not stop.

Lights blinked on in nearby homes. Distantly a car alarm triggered. Charlie's howl poured into the night causing porch lights to flicker on, as far as a mile away.

All the dogs knew the myth of the "Shiba scream," but until this night it was just another mystery of Charlie's ancestry. Stories were told of the Shiba Inu who sirened, in times of great danger, to warn the Samurai and frighten their enemies. All the dogs knew what Charlie wanted. They would not be able to wait for the coast guard to arrive.

As Charlie's scream began to fade, the crunching sound of splintering glass sharpened the air. Vader deliberately withdrew his head, like a

The wild sound exploded from his mouth.

battering ram, from the headlight he had smashed. Flint followed suit and now both headlights were dark. The poachers stood trembling but defiantly together, weapons at the ready. Hank and Rocky circled warily, at a short distance, watching for sharp rocks. Slowly, ever so slowly, Vader turned to face the poachers. Like a gate sliding open, his lips drew back, exposing rows of gleaming teeth. A deep gash on his forehead dripped blood over his nose and down onto those teeth. Flint did not look recognizable. Paint flakes had turned his face white and hundreds of crushed glass shards protruded from his fur like quills.

"We need distraction and confusion. Now!" said Vader in a low growl.

Hearing, but not understanding the growl, the poachers stiffened and Squeaky raised his knife.

Rushing in, Hank and Rocky began a coordinated game of tag, simultaneously snapping and barking. Each advance was close enough to cause the men to stumble back for a second but not close enough to come within reach of the club or knife.

"It's a bad dream. Wake up Squeaky, WAKE UP! WAKE UP," screamed Squeaky.

"Squeaky! Snap out of it!" said Tex. There's gonna be someone here any minute to call 'em off. Hold it together!"

"I don't see any humans! Where are the dog owners?" said Nitro in response, eyes following the moving dogs.

It quickly became impossible for the poachers to keep all the dogs in view. Not far from the truck, they could see Flint as he dropped low and flexed his muscles for attack.

"Where's that German Shepherd?" Nitro searched in the confusion of noise and motion.

Crouching below eye level, beneath the circling dogs, Vader slid along the sand. His training commanded him to stay flat as if a dangerous tripwire ran just above his head. He knew that surprise was the best weapon against a knife.

Vader arrived. A terrifying wolf among sheep, he launched himself up and into the midst of the poachers. He gripped Squeaky's arm for a moment and the knife fell to the ground. In seconds, Flint was by Vader's side. With all his massive strength, he railroaded Nitro, tossing the big man as if he were a small toy. Horrified and overcome, Tex tottered backward alone. That is when the rest of the dogs moved in, tightly surrounding the poachers.

FIRST TIME

Responding to frantic 911 calls about a "terrible screaming sound," the coast guard arrived at the beach just as the sky brightened to dawn. The last of an enormous hatch of green turtles was flipping happily along the beach and into the sea. Colorful surfboards lay on the beach with an assortment of discarded lanterns. Large nets and empty plastic bins littered the area around a Dodge pickup with broken headlights. Three men, clearly poachers, huddled together on the wet sand. They were ringed by snarling dogs. The men cowered, totally defeated, wet, and afraid. Two damp Labs, a Hound, twin Dalmatians, and a Bulldog, crouched around the circle. A massive Rottweiler lay partially on top of one of the men and growled threateningly. The whole group was cinched tight, by a focused Australian Cattle Dog. Just a bit separated from the others, a German Shepherd held a sharp knife trapped beneath a powerful paw. A black cat drifted, in and out of sight, prowling the tree line.

Cap and his partner Joe climbed slowly out of their truck. Cap looked neither angry nor weary this morning. He looked hopeful.

Joe stared, his eyes wide with disbelief.

"What the heck . . . what happened here?" he said rubbing his forehead with confusion.

"Don't know for sure Joe," said Cap. "Never seen anything like it. Funny thing is, these dogs, I recognize a lot of 'em from the harbor."

"Huh. You're right. I've definitely seen those Dalmatians at the gas station. They're a long way from home."

Cap and Joe advanced toward the men on the ground. The dogs drifted back, away from the poachers, but still close.

"Hey Cap!" Joe hesitated in front of Drucker then reached out to stroke him. " I recognize this one too. Local surfer. Know the man who trained him," he said.

Cap did not respond as his eyes rested on Vader. "This one is a regular around my boat. Looks like he cut himself and there's glass in his fur. Something else too, white chalk or maybe paint," he said, trailing off as he looked over at the white Dodge, headlights smashed.

The inspection continued. An electric lantern, still glowing, lay against a surfboard. Even from a distance, the brightness of its light forced Cap to look away after a minute. He turned over one of the discarded bins and a captive baby turtle streaked away. It headed straight toward the lantern and then to the waves beyond. A momentary green spot in the foam and it disappeared. Cap stared, as the pieces of the puzzle began to fit together.

"Look at these sorry excuses for criminals, huh Cap?" said Joe.

Cap nudged a surfboard with his boot but said nothing.

"Rough night, lads?" asked Joe grinning down at

the three men. "Plan didn't go as expected, maybe?"

Then, "These dogs have protected the green turtle hatchings, without any help from us," said Cap more to himself than to his partner.

"Yup," said Joe rubbing his hands together. "These guys picked the wrong beach on the wrong night. I've never seen poachers with more ridiculous bad luck and . . . "

"I don't think we are talking about luck here, Joe," interrupted Cap, "Ambush is the word that comes to mind. Land and sea. How else can we explain lanterns, surfboards, broken headlights, and these dogs, here at dawn, so far from home?"

A sudden strangled squawk interrupted Cap.

"Red fox . . . red fox," said Squeaky in a high voice, "He's out there. Watching."

"What's that you're trying to say, fella?" said Joe cupping one of his ears. "What was that? You got outfoxed tonight?" he asked, and grinning, he gestured to the watchful circle of dogs.

Joe pulled the poachers to their feet. One by one he snapped on handcuffs. Squeaky and Tex walked miserably to the coast guard truck with Joe close behind. Then it was Nitro's turn.

"Hey, I can't wear these handcuffs, they're too tight," he protested. Joe paid no attention as he pushed Nitro in the direction of his fellows.

Staring at Squeaky for a moment, Cap turned back to the waves. His heart told him what he would see. A flash of red caught his eye at the water's edge. Unnoticed, out on the beach, lay a single small dog. He did indeed look like a red fox. At that moment, his white paws were carefully crossed as he faced the handcuffed poachers, his back to the baby turtles he protected. Face alert, his almond eyes looked as if someone had traced a thick black crayon around each of them.

Cap's breath caught as he recognized Charlie. Realization dawned. He understood this moment, and, for the very first time, years of moments. Charlie and Cap shared a burden. They were both pledged to protect the unprotected. Slowly, with dignity, Captain Kegun Hatsukami bent forward. He leaned toward the sand in a formal bow of

Slowly, with dignity, Captain Kegun Hatsukami bent forward.

profound respect. He bent deeply to Charlie, as a warrior would have bowed to an honored fellow warrior, back in the time of the Samurai, and the Palace of the Sun.

Charlie bowed his head in return. The rising sun warmed the sand and a new day. Charlie's heart filled with peace as the last of the green hatchlings tumbled over his legs and tail and scampered into the surf.

*The rising sun warmed the
sand and a new day.*

CPSIA information can be obtained
at www.ICGtesting.com
Printed in the USA
LVHW051948031220
673138LV00028B/4145

9 781977 231062